Bustin' Loose

THE CACTUSVILLE KIDS

AVAILABLE BOOKS:

The Red-Hot Pepper Fiasco
Bustin' Loose

THE CACTUSVILLE 🌵 KIDS

Bustin' Loose

PATRICIA HICKMAN
Illustrated by Taia Morley

Augsburg
MINNEAPOLIS

BUSTIN' LOOSE

Library of Congress Cataloging-in-Publication Data

Hickman, Patricia.
    Bustin' loose / Patricia Hickman ; illustrated by Taia Morley.
        p.   cm.   -- (The Cactusville kids)
    Summary: Moon Holly enters the rodeo hoping to win enough money to buy
the pony she's been training, but when all her plans are thwarted, her trust in God
is the only thing that helps.
    ISBN 0-8066-2738-7
    [1. Rodeos--Fiction. 2. Ponies--Fiction. 3. Horses--Fiction.
4. Christian life--Fiction.] I. Morley, Taia, ill. II. Title.
III. Series: Hickman, Patricia. Cactusville kids.
PZ7.H53145Bu   1995
[Fic]--dc20
                                                                            95-30756
                                                                                 CIP
                                                                                  AC

The paper used in this publication meets the minimum requirements of American
National Standard for Information Sciences—Permanence of Paper for Printed
Library Materials, ANSI Z329.48-1984.   ∞

Manufactured in the U.S.A.   AF 9-2738

99   98   97   96   95   1   2   3   4   5   6   7   8   9   10

To my daughter, Jessica. Your servant's heart shines through like a beacon in the darkness. Hold to your integrity like a tiger, love.

Contents

Moon River

I never would have believed it if someone would
have told me a year ago that Moon Holly Soileau
("Swallow")—that's me—would be playing house-
keeper to fourteen half-ton, snorting, whinnying,
spoiled beasts. But I couldn't help myself. You see, I
had fallen head over heels for a pony named Glitter.
She was a POA (Pony of the Americas) who was
boarded at the Agape Stables in Cactusville, Arizona.
I had decided to try and save every penny I could
so I could one day buy Glitter from Buck, the owner
of the stables. Some days it seemed like it would
be impossible.

Now, I'm sure you might be asking yourself what a
cool kid like myself would be doing living in a place
like Cactusville, Arizona. My mom and I once lived in
Los Angeles, California, where I was a kid actress.
But I started getting sick with asthma, and the next
thing you know Mom was moving us away from the

city life. Suddenly, there we were—planted in the middle of Cactusville. What a trip!

With an old pitchfork in my hand, I scooped up a big wad of hay and tossed it onto the floor of the stall. Yesterday was the last day of school. Now the summer stretched before me like a great yawning creature that threatened to swallow me up with boredom if I didn't keep busy.

My friends Jess, Bets, and I were all working at the stables. We had to work our fingers to the bone every morning if we wanted to ride horses by the afternoon. But they had different plans for their money. They were both saving to go to some fancy dude ranch for two weeks. They would have to go without me. My money was all for Glitter.

Jess turned and made a crabby face at me when the straw I threw scattered all over her boots. "Thanks a lot, Moon Holly!" she said sourly. She was my blonde-haired friend who kept me out of trouble for the most part. Since I once did some acting in Hollywood, I called Jess my "stand-in" mom.

"All right, you two." Bets finished braiding her hair, which hung down past her western belt. "Let's get busy. I don't want to spend the whole day cleaning out Buck's stables. Don't you want to ride today?" Bets placed a bucket of water at the feet of a brown quarter horse named Martyr's Reign—we called her Marty—who was about to foal. Bets patted Marty and rubbed her huge stomach. "Her baby's due in a week or two. I'll bet it'll be gorgeous." Bets was gorgeous—and super cool.

The three of us were the best friends in the whole world. Together we had formed a secret club we called "The Cactusville Adventure Club." No boys could be in our club. Not even cute ones.

"I want to ride!" I said rather anxiously. "Let's hurry!" I had spent the whole week before in bed with the flu. I had been wrapped up in polyester sheets for so long, my hair had become one big, nasty clod of tangles on the back of my head. It took my mom a solid day—at least it seemed that way—to comb out all the mess from my shoulder-length, brown hair. I had spent a lot of time gritting my teeth and moaning. At one point I thought Mom would have to shave my head. Now, *that* would have been a new look!

More than anything, though, I missed Glitter. I was afraid that by the time I got well, she wouldn't remember me. "Later on, I need to brush down Glitter before we ride," I said. "She's probably a mess."

"Not really," Bets answered in a matter-of-fact tone. "Buck has a new stable hand named Lance River who took care of Glitter while you were sick."

"He's kind of cute, Moon." Jess wound her long, blonde hair around a finger. Her green eyes squinted in a sneaky sort of way.

I scowled. I didn't need any crackpot by the name of Lance River taking care of Glitter. "How old is he?" I asked, annoyed at the thought.

"He's thirteen—too old for you," Bets grinned as she raked the clean, yellow straw into a flattened heap on the clay floor.

Now, I was almost eleven but a confirmed bachelorette. To me, boys were usually nothing but trouble—like those two goofy nerds, Elmer Higgins and Todd Tweetweiler, who were always nosing around trying to ruin my day. This Lance River kid was probably no different from those guys. "I didn't say I wanted to marry him, did I?" I could see that Bets was trying to annoy me by the quirky smile on her face.

"That would be a laugh!" Jess opened the gate to go to the next stall. "Then we'd have to call you Moon River!"

I tried to keep a straight face while my two loony friends laughed hysterically. They tried to croon a corny old song about a moon river. Soon my quivering lips gave way and I had to giggle. "Moon River!" I exploded in laughter. "Give me a break!" Taking a deep breath, I looked toward Glitter's stall and sighed. My stomach had butterflies. My friends could tease all they wanted, but I couldn't help but wonder if this Lance character was trying to come between me and Glitter.

Dango and the Daffy Desperadoes

I f we don't take a break, I might pass out!" I complained as loudly as I could to Jess and Bets.

We walked over to the water cooler to grab a quick drink. I saw a couple of men leaning against the fence to the paddock. Their jeans were faded and frayed, and they stood slurping on root beer. They were laughing loudly and slapping their knees.

My brow must have wrinkled in a peculiar way because Bets began to explain, "They're rodeo clowns. They travel all over the U.S.—wherever there's a rodeo. You ought to see them in their clown makeup. They're hysterical!"

"They get paid for being clowns?" I couldn't believe it. "Easy money if you ask me."

"Not really." Bets gulped down the cold water and crinkled the paper cup in her hand. "They save a lot of lives."

"How could a clown save lives?" I wondered aloud.

"Well, they do all the usual silly stuff clowns do, Moon, but if a cowboy gets in trouble, they run out into the arena and help him out."

"I saw a cowboy getting chased by a wild bull once," Jess added. Her eyes were big. "Three clowns ran out into the arena and started waving huge hand-kerchiefs at the bull. He turned, snorted, and started stampeding toward the clowns. While the bull chased the clowns around in circles, the cowboy jumped up and ran away to safety."

"I don't know." I shook my head. "It still sounds like easy money to me." I had seen a lot of stunt peo-ple at work when I was signed up as an "extra" with the Starlight Talent Agency in L.A. Stunt people never had to memorize lines like the rest of us, and they only got called up for the action scenes.

"Like the time I was playing a school kid on the pioneer show 'Little Tykes of the West,'" I said launch-ing into one of my old Hollywood stories. "Each of us from the Starlight were supposed to jump out of our seats at just the right time in a spooky-looking, one-room schoolhouse, which was supposedly on fire. We had to do the scene eight times to get it right. The hero, Blaze Fiker, was supposed to charge up on his trusty steed Bolo and rescue us through the window."

Bets laughed as I bent over, riding an imaginary charger.

"But this was too dangerous for a star, so the director would scream, 'Cut!' at just the right moment. Then a skinny stunt man would come tearing through the fake tumbleweeds and jump on Bolo's back so he could ride into the blazing inferno just as the roof caved in!"

Jess gasped, while Bets just looked at me doubtfully.

"Except the roof didn't really cave in on him. They just made it look that way. Hubie Hoffmeister, my wacky Hollywood agent, had said it was 'Easy money, kid!'"

As we threw our paper cups into an old, rusted banana barrel that Buck used for a garbage can, I could hear the rodeo clowns talking about the upcoming Cactusville Rodeo.

"It'll be a lot of money for some lucky kid, Red," said the one with skin as black as coal.

"I'll say!" said the other, whose face was sunburned and whose nose was peeling. "That's one of the biggest amounts of prize money I've ever seen offered to rodeo contestants—to rodeo kids anyway."

Kids? They certainly had my attention. "Excuse me, sirs?" I tried to use my most polite voice. Even clowns deserve respect.

"What is it, little darlin'?" the one with dark skin answered. He talked like a real cowboy.

"What prize money are you talking about?"

Bets and Jess craned their ears to listen.

"The prize money for the competition for junior cowpokes," the man explained. "By the way, I'm Dango the Clown," he said. "An' this here feller's my ol' pardner, Red. We run a rodeo clown outfit called Dango and the Daffy Desperadoes. We travel all over America."

"Nice to meet you both." I shook their hands. "I'm Moon Holly, and these are *my* pardners, Bets and Jess."

The girls grinned like two pigs in a buttermilk bath when they heard me talk "cowpoke-talk." Hubie Hoffmeister would have simply died if he'd heard me!

"How much will the winner of the competition earn?" Bets asked. She reached to pick up the broom when she spied Buck tromping through the paddock.

"The prize money is one thousand dollars," Dango answered, his bristly eyebrows making a bridge over his dark brown eyes.

I nearly fainted. "One thousand dollars?"

Dango and Red nodded as they tweedled straws between their teeth.

"I could buy Glitter," I muttered to myself.

"Moon!" Jess was ecstatic. "You could buy Glitter!"

"That's what I said." I was still mumbling. My brain was already in fast forward. I could just see myself in that arena—flying around those barrels, roping calves, bowing to the cheering crowd with people screaming my name at the top of their lungs!

"I'll bet your mom would make you put the money in your college fund."

I shook myself from the fantastic daydream. "What? Who said that?"

"I did, Moon," Bets smiled in a really sheepish way. "You know your mom. She's still pretty upset with you for exploding Aunt Bert's hot peppers all over Cactusville."

"Are you going to keep bringing up all that stuff?"

I couldn't believe Bets' memory. Besides, the peppers weren't all over Cactusville, just Aunt Bert's backyard. It was an accident, and Aunt Bert had said she forgave me.

"No, but your mom will. I'm sure of it."

As usual, Bets was right. God had certainly taught me to be honest with Mom after that fiasco. "But if I work really hard, maybe she'll give in."

"I hope you work harder than you're working today." Buck had walked up on our conversation. He was huffing and puffing, and his leather boots were coated in barnyard bonanza. Phew!

Jess, Bets, and I wheeled around with our cheeks red.

"What can I say?" I shrugged my shoulders. "You caught us red-handed, Buck, falling down on the job again."

"Hey, Buckaroo, what's up?" Dango held out his gigantic hand to Buck, who slapped him "a five."

"Caught you clowning around with my hired help, eh, Dango?" Buck cocked his straw hat back on his head to wipe his forehead.

"We were just telling the cowgirls here about the upcoming rodeo. Moon Holly seems to be anxious to enter the competition." Dango pointed at me good-naturedly. "Said she wants to buy a pony."

"Glitter." Buck shook his head. "I guess Moon'll never give up until that pony is hers once and for all."

"You got it!" I smiled.

"Say, Buck," Jess had that scheming look in her eyes again. "Could you help Moon train Glitter for the rodeo?"

Buck sighed while the pail, now emptied of grain, dangled loosely from his fingertips.

I looked up at him with my best begging, puppy-dog eyes.

"Oh, for crying out . . ."

I smiled.

"All right! If you'll really work hard, I suppose I can help you."

"Hurrah!" we all cheered.

"Thank you, Buck!" I hugged him, sweaty shirt and all.

Buck held me out at arms' length and pointed his grubby finger in my face. "But it's only eight weeks away, Moon. Glitter will need a training session every day, young lady, except Sunday."

"I'll be here," I promised as I crossed my heart.

The Tag-Along

I was up at dawn the next morning. The Arizona sun was hiding just behind the mountain range, making the eastern sky look like pink icing.

I had been honest with Mom about the rodeo the night before. She was more worried about me getting hurt than anything else. I had told her so many wild stories to hide my schemes in the past that I think she must have been surprised when I spilled my guts about the rodeo. But she finally said I could try out if I promised to be really careful. It felt cool being honest.

Buck was already at the stables when I arrived on my bike. I could see his ten-gallon hat bobbing beyond the split-rail fence. He had a water hose and was spraying down the sidewalk in front of his office while giving the grasshoppers a morning shower. "Morning, Moon." He greeted me, and then grabbed a disposable coffee cup from the hood of his truck.

I yawned and rubbed the morning grunge from my eyes. "Morning, Buck." I tried to sound cheerful.

"I'd like for you to meet one of my new hands." Buck waved for the boy to come from around the office where he had been feeding the horses. "This fellow is Lance River."

I stopped dead in my tracks. Not because Lance was as cute as Jess had said he was, or because he had perfectly blue eyes, or even because of the cool way his hair hung over one eye from under his felt hat. I just wasn't counting on anyone else being around when I was trying to train Glitter. I mean, I was already short on time, and this Lance dude—well, he probably was a know-it-all anyway. I decided to give him the cold shoulder. "Hi," I said coolly, so as not to encourage him in any way.

He grinned a big smile that probably would have given Jess goose pimples, but not me. I wasn't falling for no two-bit urban cowboy. He probably wasn't even from Arizona.

Lance extended his hand, which I happened to notice was gloved with some pretty expensive leather. "Nice to meet you, Moon. I've heard a lot about you. Glitter's a fine pony."

I nodded, but all the while pretended to stare down at the grasshoppers, which by now were doing the backstroke along the cracks in the sidewalk.

Buck swigged down the last drop of his coffee and wiped his mouth with the back of his hand. "Let's get to work."

Let's? I thought. As in . . . let us? "Buck," I tried to whisper so Lance wouldn't hear. "Is *he* coming? I mean, what if I mess up in front of . . ."

"Who? Lance?" Buck chuckled in that corny way that reminded me of an old Roy Rogers movie. "Why this boy is the finest horse trainer I've ever seen. He can whip a rodeo horse and rider into shape faster'n you can shake a stick!"

I followed behind Buck and Lance, feeling like a tag-along sister. Things had been going so well for me and Glitter. Why did a second-rate hombre like Lance have to come along and spoil everything?

Pony Spies

My feelings about Lance were right on target. From the minute I led Glitter out into the paddock, that wet-behind-the-ears cowpoke was right on our tail, yelling out commands and telling me every move to make. If I'd had a boxing glove, I would have beaned him right on his know-it-all head.

"Watch your position," his voice squeaked as I rounded a barrel. "You're leaning too far out. Go with your pony. Lean with her, not against her."

His voice was grating against my ten-year-old nerves. From the fresh crop of zits across his forehead, I decided his voice change must have been pretty recent. Great! I grumbled to myself. Of all the trainers in the world, I get stuck with the teenage-mutant-walking-hormone!

"You're doing a great job, Lance!" Buck said to his new prodigy. "I'll just go in and fix myself another cup of coffee. You keep working with Moon." Buck walked out of the paddock gate.

"Sure thing, Buck," Lance said waving his hand. "She's a cute little kid."

Cute? Little? I'd show ol' Flivver or Liver or whatever-his-name-was a thing or two about real riding! I dug my heels into Glitter's flanks. "Hyah!" I yelled with all the determination of Annie Oakley.

Glitter charged around the turn kicking red dust clear into the ozone.

"Too fast!" I heard Lance shriek as my knees weakened.

All at once, as Glitter whipped around the barrel, my fingers slipped from the reins and I fell from the saddle. I ricocheted across the ground like a BB off a tin plate! When my back pockets hit the dirt, I gritted my teeth trying not to howl.

Lance streaked across the paddock and reached down to lift me up with his long arms. "You okay, little Moon?"

I would have given anything to be anywhere but there at that moment. "Uh-huh," I groaned, too embarrassed to rub where it hurt the most.

He lifted me from the ground and pulled my right arm around his neck so I could hobble back to Buck's office. I looked like a wounded bird. But my posterior wasn't the only thing that was wounded. My self-respect was lying back there in the middle of that paddock wanting to run away.

"What in the world happened?" Buck said, running out of his office when he spied us through the window.

"I fell, Buck. No big deal," I fibbed. Yanking my arm from around Lance, I dusted off the seat of my pants.

"I think she's all right, Buck," Lance added, like I knew he would. "She's a little shook up."

"What happened?"

I waited, knowing Lance couldn't wait to blab about my dumb blunder.

"I'm not really sure." He bit his lip. "Just one of those things."

Why did he say that? I wondered suspiciously. "Well, Buck," I said, "if you don't mind, I think I'll just do my own training from now on. Lance taught me a lot, but I'll just take it from here."

I had to look away from Lance. You would have thought that I had punched him in the stomach, the way he looked at me. He didn't say a word or snitch on me like I thought he would. He just stared at me with those suffering, blue eyes.

"I understand" was all he could think to say. He turned on his black Dingo heels and walked away toward the stables.

I felt like an absolute moron standing there. Buck patted my shoulder, but it didn't help matters.

"Did Lance cause you any problems, Little-bit?"

I shook my head. "No, sir."

"If you think you should do this alone, then go ahead, I guess."

"Thanks, Buck." Trying to smile, I limped toward the paddock where Lance had tied Glitter. I tried to give myself a pep talk. It was like auditioning for a commercial. I just had to give it my best shot. I had to think like a champion. I didn't need anyone else. But if that were true, why did I feel like the world's biggest jerk?

Glitter nickered as I patted her neck. "We can do it, girl. Me and you together, we don't need any Lance River to help us, do we?" I tried to sound convincing.

Little did I know that just beyond the paddock, hiding under the parents' bench, were two grubby-faced spies—Elmer Higgins and Todd Tweetweiler. They were the two meanest hombres this side of the mesas, especially Elmer. Folks around Cactusville said that if a contest were held between Elmer and a rattlesnake to see who was meanest, Elmer would win hands down.

Watching me between the fence posts, Elmer squinted his yellowish eyes while Todd lay next to him on his stomach, popping pistachios into his mouth. Todd was propped up on his elbows, his little, pointy, bird lips crunching away on the nuts.

"Quiet!" Elmer elbowed Todd, who then fell face first into the dirt.

"Ow!" Todd tried to push himself back up, spitting out dirt from between his teeth. "Watch out!" He groaned and rubbed his sore chin. "What did I do, anyway?"

"You have to be quiet if you're going to spy with me! Old radar-ears Moon Beam will hear you if you're not careful."

"Why are we spying now anyway? I could have slept late this morning. Mom was making grits."

"Yuk!" Elmer spat disgustedly. "I'd rather eat dirt!"

"I just did!" Todd checked his sore spot for any signs of blood. "I'd rather have grits!"

"Quiet! Or I won't let you be a spy anymore!" Elmer eyed Glitter's hooves as I rounded another barrel. "Now listen, Tweetweiler. We've an assignment to carry out. Moon Beam wants to win the prize money in the Cactusville Rodeo. But that prize money is going to no one else but yours truly."

Todd scratched his head. "You mean me?" He grinned a really goofy smile.

"No, Mr. Beans-for-brains. Me! But I have a secret plan for keeping Moon out of the picture."

"What?"

"When she leaves, we'll sneak back and train that old pony of hers ourselves."

Now Todd was really confused. "We're going to help her?"

"No!" Elmer's face was beet red. "We'll train the pony to do all the wrong things."

"We can do that?"

"Of course we can, Tweetweiler. We can sneak back tonight when no one's around. They don't call me Wild Bill Elmer for nothing."

"Who calls you that name, Elmer?" Todd didn't have a clue.

"Everybody! Now be quiet!"

Glitter was beginning to look tired, and both of us were sweating. I decided to walk her for a while, hose her down, and then take her back to her stable to rest. If I had known about Tweedle-dumb and Tweedle-even-dumber hiding under the bench, I would have hosed them down instead. But I didn't know. So off I rode on my bike to search for Bets and Jess, while leaving Glitter at the mercy of the weirdo pony spies.

Marty's Surprise

Casting an eerie glow over the stables, a lantern swayed through the paddock gate. The moon was full and hung in the night sky like a big lemon pie. Surrounded by the fresh hay that we had given them, the horses were snug in their stalls. Marty shifted restlessly, her belly swaying like a sack of potatoes. Glitter snorted and pawed at the floor. She must have sensed something was up.

A mop of red hair followed by two beady eyes popped up in front of the stall door. "Nice little pony. Easy does it, Trigger." Elmer said.

"It's not Trigger, it's Glitter," Todd chided.

Glitter backed away from the door and nickered nervously.

"Good little horsey. Come to El-mer!" Elmer shook a carrot at her while unlatching the gate.

Glitter shook her mane, her tail swishing the floor like a broom.

Todd held the bridle and reins in his sweaty little fingers. "Take it easy, Glitter." He tried to sound calmer than Elmer. He stepped slowly toward the pony, easing the bridle toward her nose.

Glitter bobbed her head around and snorted again while Todd patted her neck. "I got it, Elmer!" Todd felt triumphant as he slid the metal bit between the pony's teeth.

After Todd fastened the bridle around Glitter's ears, Elmer grabbed the reins. "Come on, you old nag! We're going for a riding lesson. Let's go saddle her up, Todd."

Within minutes those two scoundrels had *my* pony out in the paddock, running around in the moonlight.

They worked with her—shouting commands over and over in her ear. But they were able to get the pony to respond to only one of their kooky orders.

After working for over an hour, Todd yawned sleepily. "I have to go home, Elmer. My mom's going to be upset if she finds me missing from my bed."

"Who cares? Parents get over it."

"No, really. I vote we put Glitter back in her stall. Besides, this place is giving me the creeps."

Suddenly a piercing cry swept through the paddock. It was so loud it sent a chill up the boys' spines. Glitter stepped backward and bobbed her head nervously.

"What was that noise?" Elmer's eyes were wide.

"I don't know, Elmer, but I told you we better get out of here!" Todd looked as though he would cry. "It sounds like a ghost!"

Again, the shrill noise screeched through the stables.

"It's coming from over there!" Todd pointed toward the stables.

"I'm getting out of here!" Elmer slid out of Glitter's saddle, his goofy, blue cowboy boots stirring the dust as he jumped onto the ground.

"We can't leave this pony wandering around the paddock all night wearing a saddle, Elmer. She'll get saddle sores!"

"*You* take her back! My mom is probably looking for me." Elmer ran for the gate.

"Elmer Higgins! You come back here now and help me this instant!" Todd wailed as the frightening sound became even more distinct.

Elmer disappeared into the darkness of the night, leaving behind nothing but a cowardly trail of dust.

"That rat-fink!" Todd's forehead wrinkled as he listened again to the noise. It was beginning to sound familiar. Todd led Glitter slowly through the gate toward the stables. As he neared the stable stalls he could hear one of the horses whinnying something fierce!

"Marty!" Todd gasped, remembering about the quarter horse. Tying Glitter quickly to a hitching post, he ran to Marty's stall.

As he looked inside, he could see the mare lying on the straw. Her eyes were closed, and the straw was damp all around her flanks. She whinnied again in that spooky way.

"Oh, no! She's having her baby! What do I do?" Todd ran one way and then the next. His foggy brain was confused—he couldn't think straight!

Then, suddenly, an idea struck like lightning. "I'll go for help!" he decided, and he leaped up onto Glitter's back.

"Hi-ho, Glitter!" Todd shouted. But Glitter meandered off at her usual, slow, pony pace. "Go, horsey, go!" Todd hollered, forgetting Elmer's command for giddyap. Todd scratched his head. "Oh, I remember now! Stay, Glitter!"

Glitter whinnied loudly and tore off across the field for Buck's house just beyond the hill ahead. As they neared the crest of the hill, Todd could see the silhouette of a big man coming toward them on a four-wheeler. His wheels popped up and over the hill while his engine revved, frightening the wits out of Glitter. The pony reared in the air, sending Todd tumbling onto the dry grass.

"Owww!" Todd howled like a wounded animal.

Glitter turned and trotted back toward her stall with her reins dragging through the grass.

"What in tarnation?" Buck sounded angry. He held up his rifle just enough to let the moonlight glint off the barrel.

"Buck, it's me, Todd. D-don't shoot! P-please don't shoot!" he begged.

"Todd Tweetweiler!" Buck lowered his gun. "Do you want to get yourself shot?"

Todd began babbling as though he had lost his mind. M-m-mar! Ma-mar! Ma—B—bay—"

Buck pulled the boy up by his collar. Todd's body dangled helplessly, and he looked scrawny as a plucked chicken.

"I was chasing a fox out of my hen house, and what do I find instead but a little rat," said Buck. "What are you doing out here riding one of our animals this late at night?"

"That's what I've been trying to tell you, Buck!" Todd yelled, his voice cracking. "It's Marty! She's having her baby!"

"Marty!" Buck looked toward the stables. "I didn't think she was due for another couple of weeks. Todd, you go back and get my wife, Hannah. She can call and get another stable hand out here to help me."

"You want me to help, Buck?"

"No, Todd. If you'll get Glitter back in her stall and unsaddled for the night, then you better go on home. This could be a long night."

Welcome, Prince Ivy

My telephone rang early the following morning. It was Jess.

"Moon!" She sounded breathless. "You have to come to the stables right away!"

"What's wrong?" I tried to gulp down a sloppy bite of shredded wheat.

"It's Marty! She's having her baby. She should foal at any minute. Buck and Lance have been up with her all night."

"I'll be right there!" I hung up the phone and ran to throw on my grungiest jeans and a denim shirt.

When I raced through our house, Mom was on the floor "stretching out her flab" as she calls it, before starting her morning aerobics. "Where are you going, Moon?" she asked between puffs, smashing her nose against her knee.

"I have to hurry, Mom! Marty's having her baby. I have to go help her!"

"Who?" Mom's face would wrinkle up like a raisin sometimes.

Throwing open the door, I yelled back in a hurry, "It's Marty! She's in labor!"

"Moon, you'll be in the lady's way . . ." She tried to yell after me, but I was already leaping on my bike when she shrieked, "You can't deliver a baby! Moon!"

When I pedaled into the stables, my friends' bikes were already parked out front. I found Bets and Jess with anxious faces standing outside Marty's stable.

"You made it!" Jess patted my back.

"Look inside, Moon," Bets pointed toward the stall.

I gripped the stall gate and found Buck and Lance kneeling beside Marty. And then, for the first time in my life, I actually watched a colt being born.

The newborn foal was black and wet-looking. Its head and one front leg were already showing. Buck held its front leg and was pulling it down toward Marty's hind leg. Lance switched places with him as Buck guided him through the birthing.

"When Marty starts pushing again, just take the foal's front leg and curve it down around Marty's backside," he instructed.

Lance focused on Buck's words, carefully following each command he was given. "Pull the foal around? You mean, as in a circle?"

"That's right," Buck answered in a gentle tone. "That way it will be born right next to its mama. It makes the newborn feel secure."

Marty whinnied loudly then groaned as she began pushing again.

"Now, Lance!" Buck smiled. "Go!"

Lance dug his knees into the pile of straw and pulled firmly on the foal's leg. Suddenly, the second leg popped out, and Lance guided it around Marty's flank. Marty shook her head and glanced around at the foal, who was already struggling to stand with his wobbly front legs. Pretty soon his flanks appeared. After pushing a few more times, Marty's son was born!

The little colt sat in the pile of straw, his eyes sparkling up at us. He shook his ears, and the water that had kept him safe in his mother's womb for all those months splattered all over Lance and Buck. Marty turned her head and nickered at the colt, her brown eyes gleaming.

Bets looked at him dreamily. "I knew he would be gorgeous. He's a little miracle—just like all babies."

"What do you mean?" I asked.

"Look at him, Moon. Could *you* create anything so beautiful?"

I studied the colt's face and laughed as he tried to stand on his wobbly, long legs. "No way! People can't make their own horses."

"Only God can." Bets just kept gazing into the stall and mooning over the new arrival.

Bets was so . . . well, holy acting. I never would have thought of those things before I met her. But slowly I was beginning to understand about God and about being a Christian. But Bets, she could see God in everything.

"He's another little gift from God," Buck chuckled as the foal collapsed onto an ivy vine that had grown up in the corner of Marty's stall. When the foal raised its rubbery neck, the vine snapped and clung to his ears. Shaking his head at the annoyance, the colt lay with his legs sprawled, looking up at all of us in bewilderment.

We laughed at the sight of the laurel of greenery that encircled his head and dangled over one ear.

"It looks like a crown!" Jess giggled.

"That's right!" Bets added. "He's the new prince of the stables."

"That settles it, then," Buck announced while slapping his knee. "We'll call him Prince Ivy."

"Prince Ivy!" I said excitedly. "What a perfect name! I love it! It's totally awesome!"

Lance stepped away when Marty got to her feet and turned to lick her baby. Gathering up the soiled straw with a rake, Buck reached for a shovel and scooped up some stuff he called Marty's placenta. "One of you cowgirls want to scatter some fresh straw around in here for the new mother and her son while I go see Dr. Scott?"

I leaped at the chance. Throwing open the stall door, I grabbed the wheelbarrow next to us and wheeled in some more straw. "What are you going to do with him, Buck?" I asked as I heard Glitter whinnying two stalls down.

"He'll be for sale soon, just like Glitter. He'll make a good saddlebred for someone to ride and care for."

I shrugged my shoulders. He was a cute little fellow, but Glitter was going to be all mine one day. After all, I had prayed for God to give me the money for her.

"Hello there, folks!" a friendly voice said.

Buck smiled at the man who greeted him from the doorway. "Hello, Dr. Scott!" He showed the veterinarian Marty's placenta. "I wanted you to make sure everything was all right with the new mother."

Dr. Scott studied the placenta carefully.

"What is that for?" I asked, making a face at the slick-looking stuff on the shovel.

Dr. Scott explained everything to me just like I was a grown-up. "Well, Moon, just like all mammals, Marty had a sac inside of her that grew partially around her baby. It helped to nourish the colt until the day it was born. We have to make sure that the whole placenta is here. If anything were left inside Marty, it could make her sick."

"Does everything look okay, Doc?" Buck asked.

"It's all there, Buck. Marty should be just fine." Dr. Scott glanced at his watch. "I better hurry. I need to go check Ralph Bunky's cow, Rachel. She's having her calf this morning and she might need some help." Dr. Scott waved good-bye, and Buck walked him to his truck.

Turning back to my chores, I tossed straw around the floor. When I raked the straw over beside her, Marty picked at it for only a moment. Then she turned to lick Prince Ivy again. I stepped out of the way when Lance told me the colt was trying to get a drink of milk from his mother. He kept wiggling his lips all over Marty's stomach while she kept turning to lick him. His knees gave way again, and Prince Ivy dropped to the floor. Ker-plunk!

"Why won't Marty keep still, Lance?" I asked.

"She's so excited to see her colt that she wants to touch him. He can't nurse anyway until his legs get stronger."

"How soon will that be?" I wondered.

"In about an hour or so."

"I'll come back and check on him," I said. "But I need to go give Glitter a workout." I turned quickly before Lance could try to give me any advice about Glitter.

River to the Rescue

Entering Glitter's stall, I couldn't help but laugh at her. She nodded her head up and down and nickered at me. I could tell she was excited to see me. Carrots were her absolute favorite treat, so I broke one into several pieces and fed it to her. "I'll be right back, girl!" I patted her neck.

Running to the tack room, I lifted the saddle from the sawhorse and hoisted it through the door. In no time at all, Glitter was saddled up and ready to go. She shook her mane at me after I strapped on her bridle. "You act like you belong to me," I grinned at her, and she seemed to smile back at me with her eyes.

As I walked Glitter out to the paddock, I couldn't help but notice the beautiful blue sky. I thought of all the super things that were happening. A new colt had been born. Glitter would soon be mine. Everything was absolutely perfect! Today would be a great day— or so I thought.

Glitter seemed a bit jumpy at first when I mounted her. I clucked my tongue at her, and she seemed to shudder.

"Let's go, girl!" I tried to sound firm.

The pony took a few steps forward and then stood in place with her head up as though she were waiting for a signal.

"What's wrong, Glitter? Do you have a stone in your hoof?" I decided the shoe must be causing her problem. Shifting to the side of the saddle, I gave the usual command I used before I dismounted. "Stay!"

Glitter whinnied and tossed her head before leaping forward. As we streaked into the paddock, I grabbed the saddlehorn to hang on for my life. "No, Glitter!" I shrieked while fumbling for the reins again. "Stay! Stay!"

Around the barrel my pony galloped with me barely hanging on to the saddlehorn. I managed to grab one of the reins while the other one flapped around, hitting me in the ear. It stung like crazy and I wanted to cry. By now the stable hands were running into the paddock, whistling and whooping at my runaway pony. Glitter bounded past them like a racehorse while the guys jumped to get out of the way.

Without even bowing my head or closing my eyes I started praying . . . fast! If ever I needed the Lord's help, it was now!

As we whipped around another barrel, I could see the paddock gate fly open. In rode Lance on his black Arabian, Galbor. He charged toward us like the wind! Galbor was swift and long-legged and twice as tall as

Glitter. Lance galloped alongside us so he could grab Glitter's bridle. In less than a minute, Lance had brought Glitter to a halt.

"Yea!" the kids standing around the paddock all cheered. "It's River to the rescue!" one of them shouted.

My hands shook as I got down from the pony. "I don't know what happened!" My boots landed on the ground, and I was glad of it. I stared at the ground feeling embarrassed. My ear still hurt, and my arms and legs felt stiff and weak.

"You'll probably be sore tomorrow, Moon." Lance tried to sound polite. "Maybe you should give it a rest for a few days. Maybe Glitter just needs . . ."

"Needs what?" I shot back. "A new trainer?" I crossed my arms and glared at him.

"That's not what I was going to say!" Now Lance sounded angry. "I was just going to say that maybe Glitter just needs a little more time before she comes around. Some ponies are more stubborn than others." He stared down at me. "Just like some people!"

"What are you trying to say, Lance? You think *I'm* stubborn?" I may have had a tough look on my face, but inside it was as though a small voice was telling me to back off. But I couldn't stop myself. I was all ready to tear into this acne-faced cowpoke like a bull in a china shop. "I'll show you, River! You just watch Moon Holly walk away with all the prize money. I'll beat you . . . and your reject from the glue factory!"

If nothing else got to him, that statement certainly did! Lance cocked his hat over the front of his head and laughed. "You won't see Galbor in no two-bit rodeo. But I'll make you a deal. I'll get Anasazi ready, and I'll enter that rodeo contest myself!"

"Fat chance!" I shouted as he mounted the handsome Arabian horse.

Lance rode away on Galbor, while I kicked at the ground.

"Me and my big mouth!" How could I ever think that I could beat Lance River on any horse? He was the best rider and trainer I had seen. Not only that, but Anasazi was one of the stable's thoroughbreds who was already trained in calf-roping. With a little more time, Lance would have her ready for all the events. If I hadn't been so stubborn, he could have helped *me* win the prize money. A thousand dollars would be almost enough to buy Glitter. Now I had no choice. I would have to work even harder if I were ever going to have a chance of winning.

The World's Biggest Loser

I got up at the crack of dawn every morning. And as each week passed, working with Glitter seemed to get harder and harder. I had no idea she was having late-night training sessions with Elmer and Todd. Glitter actually looked tired one morning, and she didn't even want to leave her stall. What to do? We only had two days left until the Cactusville Rodeo! Yet as I looked into Glitter's big, brown eyes, I knew I couldn't be angry with her. "Come on, girl," I spoke more gently. "Let me give you a nice bath. That will perk you up."

After slipping a cloth halter over her nose, I led Glitter inside the barn where I helped bathe the horses for the owners. After hitching her inside the iron enclosure for the bath, I spent a lot of time scrubbing her neck and mane and hosing down her feet. A big scrub brush knocked the dirt off her hooves as I scraped it back and forth. From a spray can, I sprayed her hooves to make them nice and shiny. "There you go, Glitter. Nice new feet." She shifted her hooves a bit and snorted. The hoof lacquer was cold!

"I hope you feel better now." I shook my head. "A shower always makes me feel better." Sometimes I'd stay so long my fingers and toes would wrinkle. But Glitter only got shinier. "Let's go for a ride." I tried to sound hopeful.

When we arrived at the paddock, Buck was allowing in all the riders who were planning to enter the contest. Buck was speaking into a small megaphone. "Let's all take a little practice run, girls and boys. I'm going to tell you everything to expect when you arrive at the rodeo."

The megaphone squeaked and squawked as Buck turned up the sound.

"When the rodeo begins you'll hear some music from the grandstands. That's when the parade of riders will begin. You'll enter from the east gate and parade in on your steeds single file. Don't forget to wear the number they give you. The judges will be watching you from the moment you enter the gate, and that number tells them who you are. Let's get started, and remember, make Agape Stables proud. But most of all, let's make the Lord proud of our behavior and good sportsmanship."

Buck pressed down the play button on his tape player. The player cranked out some really corny parade music.

Just ahead of me was Elmer Higgins on his dad's horse, Yankee Doodle. Elmer jerked his head around and stuck out his tongue. "Good luck, Moon Beam. You're going to need it!"

"Same to you, macaroni-head!" I turned and looked away. Now I was even feeling bad about quarreling with Elmer, even though he deserved it. It just didn't feel fun anymore to throw all those great zingers at him.

Maybe those new feelings were what Bets and Jess were talking about when they said things like "The more you pray, Moon, the more your heart will begin to change."

"That prize money is as good as mine, Moon Beam! Eat my dust!" Elmer plowed his spurs into Yankee Doodle's flanks.

The quarter horse whinnied loudly and bolted into the paddock, his rear hooves kicking dust into Glitter's face. Glitter snorted and stamped her feet. I could tell her eyes stung, and so did mine.

"Now all of you keep your horses trotting along behind the one ahead of you. Good job!" Buck grinned as Glitter and I sauntered into the parade line.

Behind me I could hear the clip-clopping of Anasazi's shoes. Lance River had shown up just like he said he would.

Suddenly Glitter turned her head and looked toward the center of the arena as the music blared through Buck's cheap sound system. Snorting and neighing, she turned in the opposite direction of where I was guiding her to go. With her head held high, she tromped to the center of the arena and started lifting her front left leg and then her right one.

The kids all died laughing as I struggled to make her stop. "Whoa, Glitter!" I pleaded, my face bright red.

Glitter turned around in a circle and then started lifting her hooves again to the music.

"Look!" cried a girl I knew named Amy. She laughed and pointed as she brought her palomino, Copper, to a halt. "Moon's pony, Glitter, is dancing!"

All the kids started laughing and clapping as they gathered around me on their mounts.

"That's real cute, Moon," Buck's voice sounded annoyed. "But you can't do that at the rodeo. You'll get disqualified."

"I'm not doing it, Buck! It's Glitter. I think there's something wrong with her!"

Elmer Higgins was laughing so hard he was holding his sides. "That's the goofiest thing I've ever seen! You'll never beat us with that clown!"

I wanted to smack his face, but I didn't. I just sat there in the middle of the arena feeling like the world's biggest loser.

Dango's Plan

The entire day left me totally humiliated! It didn't seem to matter what event we practiced; Glitter would do it all wrong!

While the other riders sped around the barrels on their horses with ease, Glitter seemed to tap-dance past them. If we practiced bolting from the rider's chute to rope a calf, Glitter was up to her silly antics again, chasing down the confused calf and licking its face! If I said, "Giddyap," she stood perfectly still. When I shouted, "Whoa!" Glitter would turn around in a circle. Every single time Buck would play the grandstand music, she would start prancing back and forth again like she was in a cheap circus act!

Elmer Higgins seemed to be enjoying himself more than usual. He laughed so hard, I thought he would croak. Lance didn't say anything at all. He seemed to keep his mind mostly on Anasazi, who was making good time on most of the events.

On the side bench sat someone I had hardly noticed. He had been watching me and Glitter the whole time. Pulling out a red bandanna, the man seemed to be waving it like a flag. I looked all around me and realized he must be waving at me. I pointed to myself. "Me? You want me?"

He nodded his head up and down in a really exaggerated way.

Realizing Glitter wasn't going to do anything I asked, I clucked my tongue and said, "Stay!" And of course she galloped toward the man.

"Howdy, little buckaroo!" The man stood up, and I could see that it was none other than Dango the clown.

"Hi, Dango," I said glumly.

"That's the wackiest training I've ever seen. How did you get your pony to do all those crazy things?"

"I didn't." I shook my head. "She's doing it without my help. I don't know what to do."

"I have an idea," Dango whispered, "if you're willing to listen—and accept a change in plans."

"Sure." I shrugged my shoulders. "Why not? I have nothing left to lose."

Hunnymoon the Hilarious

The day of the Cactusville Rodeo had finally arrived! The kickoff that day was a parade right down Main Street. The streets were so full of people, you would have thought it was the Orange Bowl Parade! There wasn't a lot to do in Cactusville unless you liked to go fishing down by Gilley's Pond or wade through the creek barefoot chasing toad frogs. So a parade was a big deal to everyone and a good way to visit with folks you hadn't seen in a while.

The contestants in the rodeo rode two by two between the high school band and the town float. The float was loaded down with Wanda Weedlemier who had been crowned "Miss Cactusville," and her court of Cactusville beauties.

Jess and Bets rode with the Agape Riding Club. They were wearing their best rodeo duds, and from where I was riding in the parade, I could see them looking all around trying to find me.

"Where in the world is Moon Holly?" Bets' face looked worried.

"I don't know," Jess answered, "but she better show up pretty soon or she'll be disqualified."

"Maybe with all the trouble she's had with Glitter, she decided not to show up anyway. You know how she would rather die than be embarrassed in front of a bunch of people." Bets adjusted her turquoise hat, which matched her riding outfit.

"It just seems like she would tell us. After all, we're her best friends." Jess squinted, her eyes half noticing the rodeo clowns that led the parade.

"Let's keep looking. I know she's around here somewhere."

After the parade ended, the Cactusville Fairgrounds and Rodeo Arena filled up with people from as far away as Needles, Arizona. They seemed to gobble down anything that didn't move—and a few things that did! There were samples of all kinds of food from everyone's kitchen in town, whether they could cook or not. There were pickled eggs, deep-fried dill pickles, hot pickled peppers, and pickled "this" and pickled "that." By the time I made it through the home-cooked samples section, my lips were permanently pickled and puckered.

"Moon!" a voice from behind me said.

I turned to see Dango standing there straightening his costume. "Hi, Dango! I lost sight of you when the parade ended."

"You better come with me. I need you to help me finish up with Glitter. She's going to be great today!"

"Yes sir, sarge!" I saluted, then followed after him.

It wasn't long until all ears were turned toward the rodeo arena. Loud music blasted from the giant speakers above the stadium. People were packed into the stands, their arms loaded down with cheesy-looking stuffed animals and greasy bags of peanuts and pistachios.

I stood next to Glitter outside the clowns' dressing room. We had her dressed in a big, ruffled, polka-dot collar and a giant, straw cowboy hat. Around her big, brown eyes I had helped to paint white circles. Her saddle blanket was made of outrageously colorful woven fabric with sparkly sequins, and her hooves were painted hot pink. Glitter really glittered!

Red looked down at me with a big grin. He was dressed like a cowboy clown sheriff. "She's going to steal the show, Moon," Red laughed. "I still can't believe you gave up your only chance to win the prize money."

"It was the only right thing to do, Red."

Dango added, "Sometimes God's plans are different from our own. I'm sure some of your friends back in L.A. probably wouldn't agree with me, Moon, but if we let God lead us, all kinds of good things can happen."

I nodded but sighed at the thought of the prize money going down the drain. "I guess God's trying to teach me some things—like patience and obedience."

The announcer in the grandstands started the rodeo with a prayer for the cowboys' safety. All twelve of the clowns pulled their hats off and bowed their

heads. I did too. I wanted to thank God for the peace-
fulness I felt today, even though I didn't get my
own way.

Within moments after the prayer, we could see the
tops of the flagpoles just ahead of us as the contestants prepared to enter the arena. To the side was
Elmer Higgins getting ready to mount Yankee Doodle.
He had turned on a water hose and was drinking from
the nozzle.

The riders paraded in single file just like Buck had
shown us. I could see Lance River waving to the crowd
astride Anasazi's back. You would have thought he
was Roy Rogers by the friendly way he greeted the
audience. But I knew it wasn't right to feel jealous. I
really owed Lance a big apology.

After catching up with the rest of the riders,
Elmer Higgins came trotting behind on Yankee
Doodle, Elmer's pointy spurs clamped onto those blue
cowboy boots. I cringed at the thought of him winning
that prize money.

As the parade of contestants filed out of the arena
and right past us, the clowns mounted their horses
and waited. Glitter shifted nervously as I led her to
the rear of the clowns to prepare her for the upcoming
performance.

"Ladies and gentlemen! Boys and girls of all ages!
The Cactusville Rodeo is pleased to present the zani-
est, rip-roaringest rodeo clowns in all the world—
Dango and the Daffy Desperadoes!" the announcer
shouted as the crowd cheered.

"It's show time, gang!" Dango yelled.

I patted Glitter and whispered to her, "Let's knock 'em dead, Glitter!" Pulling myself into the saddle, I tied on the floppy hat Dango had given me and checked my shiny, red nose to be certain it was still glued on. "Surprise, Cactusville!" I laughed. I was ready for my debut as Hunnymoon the Clown!

Clowns of every size scattered around the arena, tripping and somersaulting. Some were tall and skinny, some were round, and one was even as short as me! As the clowns zipped around the course on foot, launching into their bad-guy/good-guy act, I rode Glitter around the outskirts, tossing candy to the little kids in the stands. They went nuts grabbing for the goodies and shouting for me to throw them more. They especially seemed to like the clown pony that trotted beneath me, her floppy hat wagging around her ears.

The wild-west music blared as the announcer said, "And now we present for the first time ever . . . Hunnymoon and her prancing pony, Glitter!" From the corner of my eye, I could see Jess and Bets sitting in the stands looking at one another, totally confused.

"Hunnymoon and Glitter?" Bets turned and stared at me.

"It can't be!" Jess held her hands to her face.

"Look at the girl clown, Jess." Bets' mouth fell wide open. "It's . . . it's Moon Holly!"

I flicked the on-button on the little clip-on microphone Dango had given me. As I spoke to Glitter, my voice echoed all over the arena. But I didn't use my regular voice. I had practiced the whole night before on the voice Dango had taught me to use. It was sort of like a cartoon voice I had heard on Saturday morning television.

"Now it's time for school, Glitter," my voice rang. "Let's see what a good pony you've been." I jumped off Glitter's back. "But first I need to give you a little examination." I hoped for the first time that Glitter would do all the wrong things. "Say 'ah!'"

Glitter shook her head back and forth. It looked as though she were saying, "No!"

I could hear some boys laughing from the stands behind me.

"Well, then, let's count to three." As I counted, Glitter stomped her hoof. Only she didn't stomp three times. She stomped five times!

This time the parents laughed along with the kids.

"No, not like that!" I pretended to fuss at her. "Like this!" I stomped my clown shoe three times.

I could hear the kids in the crowd counting along with me—I guess they wanted to help the poor little pony count. "One, two, three!" they shouted.

Glitter stood still, looking bored as the crowd seemed to be even more tickled at the scene.

I pulled a ruler from my back pocket. "Here, let me draw the number three for you in the dirt." I turned around and bent way over so my backside would be in front of Glitter.

Taking her cue, the pony took a step forward and punched me in the seat of the pants with her nose. I fell forward into the dust, just like Dango had trained me to do. The audience roared with laughter as Glitter stood there looking innocent.

Jumping up, I dusted the dirt off my goofy-looking pants and acted as though I was really getting steamed. Even my old Hollywood agent, Hubie Hoffmeister, would have been proud of my performance. Lifting my left foot into the stirrup, I seated myself back in the saddle. "No! No! No!" I scolded. "You're being bad, Glitter! Just for that I'm going to make you run laps. Now, giddyap!"

Glitter stood perfectly still while everyone kept laughing.

"Come on, Glitter! Giddyap!"

Glitter was great! She was bringing down the house, just like Dango and Red had said she would do.

"Okay, then, see if I care. Stay!"

Glitter took off around the arena. I let my legs fly all around, acting as though I would tumble off. The music grew loud again, and Glitter bounded for the center of the arena, where she began lifting her hooves to the music.

The crowd rose to their feet, clapping along with the music.

"Whoa!" I shouted while Glitter started turning in circles.

Just as we made another turn, I could see Elmer Higgins glaring at us from the side. "That rat-fink, Moon Beam!" he ranted and raved. *I'm* the one who trained that pony to do those things! It's *me* that should be getting the applause."

"What?" Lance had overheard the whole thing.

At that point, I think Elmer "the Fudd" Higgins must have totally lost his mind. He took off on foot running toward us. But just as he neared us, he stuck his goofy, blue boot right in the middle of some mud— mud that was caused because he had forgotten to turn off the water hose when he got a drink before the show. "I'm the trainer of that trick pony!" He shouted. "I'm the one they should be applauding for! You bring that pony over here!" He tugged at his boot.

Suddenly I had a wonderfully delicious idea. "Sure thing, little boy!" I was still Hunnymoon the Clown, and as Hubie always said, the show must go on!

Elmer turned around to yank his boot again. It made a loud sucking noise as it popped out of the mud. Then his other boot got stuck. The audience loved it! They thought he was part of the act! Elmer reached again to pull out his other foot. Bending over with his back pockets stuck right in Glitter's face, Elmer grumbled to himself.

Nickering and shaking her mane, Glitter stepped forward and bumped Elmer from behind. Elmer plunged face first into the black, gooey mud! Glitter whinnied and turned to gallop away.

The audience went wild! They waved their hats and whistled as Glitter and I paraded one last time around the arena while the clown sheriff and his clown posse dragged Elmer from the arena.

The kids really seemed to fall in love with Glitter. I was so glad that I had gone through with Dango's plan. Those smiles were worth more than a zillion dollars to me, let alone a thousand.

The music exploded over our heads. I gave the wrong command to Glitter again so she would gallop out of the arena. It was time for the rodeo competition to begin!

Bustin' Loose

As the Arizona sun began setting on Cactusville, it blazed an orange streak across the clouds. The sky looked as though it were on fire. It was gorgeous!

The floodlights around the rodeo arena began popping on one by one. Everyone felt excited as the junior contestants prepared for the competition.

Just outside the grand entrance, the guys and gals warmed up their horses in the parking lot. Inside the arena, pros were taking their turns at riding the wild bronco—Widow Maker. This wild steed was a black bronco who refused to be broken. He was jerking one cowboy around so hard the man was swung sideways from the saddle horn.

"You stay here with Glitter, Hunnymoon!" Dango yelled. Then he ran out into the arena to help the cowboy.

The arena was full of Dango's clowns, running in all directions and waving their arms at the wild stallion.

Widow Maker bucked and kicked until one of the clowns, Red, was able to grab the front of the bridle and jerk the horse's head down. The other clowns leaped toward the swinging cowboy and pulled him free from the saddle. Just then, Buck and Lance came charging out on Miss Molly and Anasazi. Buck grabbed Widow Maker's reins while Lance held his bridle. Then they led the stallion back to the paddock.

A set of long horns behind the stallion's paddock banged against the railing. Lance looked over the top of the fence and found two fierce eyes staring up at him. Anasazi neighed nervously while Lance stroked her neck. "Easy does it, girl. That old bull won't hurt you. I'll get a club and bop his head if he tries anything!"

"That's Durk's Diablo, Lance." Buck shifted in the saddle on Miss Molly. "It would take more than a club to bring Diablo down. He's a monster of a bull."

"Diablo is the Brahman from Will Durk's ranch?" Lance scratched his head. "He's even bigger than the last time I saw him."

"There hasn't been a pro yet that could stay on him." Buck turned the palomino back toward the parking lot to check on his students.

Diablo pawed the ground and slammed his horns against the paddock again. The great hump between his shoulders shifted. Anasazi whinnied and reared her front hooves off the ground.

"Whoa!" Lance pulled back her reins and backed the thoroughbred away from the paddock.

Lance rode Anasazi out toward the parking lot. He didn't notice that two blue boots were poking out from under a nearby bush. They were Elmer's boots. After Lance passed by, Elmer pulled the brush away from his face and stepped out to face the beast. "I'm not afraid of no goofy old bull," he sneered. He mimicked Diablo and pawed the soft clay with his boots.

Diablo turned his huge head toward Elmer and snorted. Elmer pointed his fingers over his head like horns and snorted back at the beast. "Take that, creep!"

The savage Brahman threw back his head and bellowed as he pawed the ground.

"Ha, ha!" Elmer snickered, then bent over and bellowed back at Diablo. He was so busy trying to act tough he didn't notice that the bull was backing away from him.

In a rage, the bull plowed toward the gate and rammed it with his head. The horns tore through the top railing, and the bull backed away to charge the rail again.

Elmer leaped backward and hollered, "Help!" Fleeing toward the concession stands, he screamed like a lunatic. "It's Diablo! He's bustin' loose!"

Women screamed and grabbed their children! Men screamed and grabbed their wives! Elmer jumped inside an old barrel! Everyone else ran for their lives! Some ran into the nearby creek, but most poured into the parking lot.

Suddenly there was a flurry of dirt and barbed-wire fence! Diablo bounded toward the stadium. He lowered his head and searched the stands for Elmer. Diablo sniffed the air and the ground warily. The fence wire dangled loosely from one of his horns.

The stands were now completely empty.

Inside the barrel, Elmer trembled and fidgeted, biting his fingernails.

The clowns and I could see people running and screaming. We didn't know about Elmer and Diablo.

"Where is everyone going?" Red stood with his hands on his hips.

Lance River came galloping across the arena toward us. "It's Diablo! He's broken free from the pen and is running loose near the stadium!"

"Here we go again! First Widow Maker acts up. Now Diablo is loose!" Dango shook his head.

"I'm going too, Dango!" I jumped up on Glitter.

"What?" Dango snapped. "I can't let a little girl go chasing off after a wild bull!"

"Let her go, Dango," Lance winked at me. "She's as tough as they come."

I couldn't help but smile at Lance. He was really an all right kind of dude.

"Moon, you go around that way and I'll go the other," said Lance. "We can cut Diablo off at the pass." He nudged Anasazi's flanks.

Dango slapped his hat against his knee. "And then what are you going to do, pray tell?"

"I don't know." Lance shrugged his shoulders. "We'll decide when we get there."

"Of all the . . ."

Dango started ranting and raving. But Lance and I galloped toward the stands to face the dreaded Diablo.

Glitter and I slowed to a walk. My hands were sweaty. Lance rounded the outside of the arena. I could see the top of his hat bobbing slowly above the arena fence. I stopped beside the flagpoles and waited for Lance's signal.

Then my eyes fell on the Brahman bull. He must have weighed nearly a ton. He pawed at the ground and sniffed all around the barrel. Catching a whiff of Elmer's scent, the bull snorted and grunted almost disgustedly.

Lance slowly began getting his lariat ready. Diablo swung his head around and prodded Elmer's hiding place with one of his horns.

A low moan came from inside the barrel. Diablo bellowed loudly! It must have scared the boots off Elmer because he let out a yelp that was heard for miles. The sound of Elmer's voice made the bull even more angry, and he charged at the barrel. The fence wire hanging from his head swung around like a whip.

A lot of things were going through my mind right about now. After all, Elmer Higgins had caused me nothing but trouble. But I was also having a change of heart. That change made me feel sorry for poor old Elmer. Being a Christian sure gave me a lot of new decisions to make. So I made one right then and there. Enemy or not, I would try to help "the Fudd."

While I was thinking about all this, the force of the bull's blow had knocked the barrel against the stands.

"Ow!" Elmer shrieked as his skinny body bounced around inside the wooden container.

I knew I had to think fast. Remembering how rodeo clowns were supposed to distract the bull so the victim could run away, I shouted to Diablo, "Hey, you!"

Diablo jerked his head around. He glared at Glitter and me. Behind him, Lance eased up quietly. Anasazi's hooves barely stirred the dust. I got my heels ready to signal Glitter as Diablo lowered his ferocious head and began pawing the ground. His eyes turned red! Then he bellowed and charged us like a Sherman tank.

"Giddyap!" I yelled. It was time to move! I dug my heels into Glitter's flanks.

But Glitter stood motionless and nickered nervously. "Oh, no!" What did I just say?

Diablo drew nearer. I could see his steely eyes zeroing in on my confused pony.

My mind went blank. What was the command for "go?" I couldn't think. We were doomed!

Diablo threw back his monstrous head as he charged around the flagpoles toward me.

"Moon!" Lance began to panic, and he and Anasazi took off after the charging bull. "Whoa, you beast!"

Suddenly Diablo's eyes grew wide as the barbed wire—which was still decorating his head—swung around one flagpole and hung on the flagpole latch. His horns were within inches of us when he was jerked back. His feet scrambled to a halt. He bellowed in Glitter's face. But Glitter just stared at Diablo curiously and craned her neck toward him. Much to Diablo's surprise, she stuck out her tongue and licked him—right on his big, ugly nose!

Lance skidded to a stop behind the bull. His mouth fell open. He had been at the stables the day Glitter had acted so weird. When I had tried to train her for calf-roping, she had licked the calf's nose. Lance threw back his head and laughed.

Behind me I could hear the galloping of horses' hooves and whooping of cowboys. Buck and the rodeo clowns surrounded us on horseback. Their lariats were flying as they tied down the bewildered Diablo. "Hold it right there, you ornery critter!" Dango fretted.

"How in the world did you snare that beast?" Buck shook his head as he wound more rope around Diablo.

"It wasn't me, Buck." I held up my hands. "It was God."

"Thank you, Lord," Buck said as he wiped his eyes.

Buck was crying! But I didn't care. I think it's okay for a cowboy to cry. Buck spends a lot of time talking about getting his strength from God. Maybe if a lot more people would learn to cry and depend on God for their strength, they would be as happy as Buck. I suddenly realized that showing we can cry is just another way of showing who the stronger ones are in this world—the ones who don't mind admitting their weaknesses. If I had been able to admit I needed help in training Glitter, I would have been ready for the rodeo competition.

It wasn't long until the bull was led away and the stands filled up again with people. Even the sight of a runaway bull couldn't keep the folks away from the big event of the evening—the presentation of the trophies and the crowning of the Cactusville Rodeo Queen!

Dango tapped my shoulder. "We better get back to our posts. We'll be needed for the finale."

"Right-o, boss!" I gave Glitter a pat on the neck and the proper command, "Whoa!" We galloped around to the grand entrance.

12

The Main Event

M oon, are you all right?" Jess came running behind
me and Glitter. Right on her heels was Bets, who
was hugging a box of popcorn to her chest. "Don't you
ever do anything like that again! You scared us to death!"

"Hi, girlfriends! Where have you been?" I smiled.

"I can't believe you faced that horrible bull, Diablo.
Were you afraid, Moon?" Bets held her fingernails to
her teeth.

I thought for a moment. I couldn't lie. "Yes . . . I
was really scared. I prayed like crazy."

We prayed too, Moon." Bets pressed her chin
against Glitter as she looked up at me with her dark
eyes. "God came through for you again, didn't he?"

I had to giggle. Bets was right, as usual.

"And now lay-dees and gentlemen!" the speakers
roared over our heads. "We are proud to announce the
main event—the winners of the Cactusville Junior
Rodeo Competition!"

The audience went wild with applause and whistling.

The music began again, and the junior competitors filed in on their horses. Lance came galloping in on Anasazi and circled all the others before reining the horse to a halt. Elmer plodded in last, his clothes coated in dirt and his face covered with Band-Aids.

One by one the winners were announced for each event and presented with a trophy. Lance won most of them. I had known he would.

The announcer shouted, "Now we are pleased to present the trophy for which you've all waited! The overall winner of the Cactusville Junior Rodeo Competition is . . ."

The stands were silent. Elmer sat slumped in his saddle while Yankee Doodle swatted flies with his tail.

". . . the best junior cowboy in all of Cactusville! Congratulations, Lance River!"

Lance looked over at me and winked as he galloped toward the grandstand to receive his award and a check for a thousand dollars. The cheers went up for the best cowboy in Cactusville. I clapped too. I was proud of him. He had worked harder his whole life than anyone I knew. And now he was a champion! But more than that—he was a real Christian. He had never put me down, even though I deserved it. He had the heart of a true servant, and I could tell that God was blessing him for it.

"We would now ask that the arena be cleared for the crowning of the Cactusville Rodeo Queen," the master of ceremonies announced.

I turned Glitter, and we went to wait at the entrance. The cowgirls were dressed in the fanciest western outfits I had ever seen. Wearing her bright pink outfit, Amy rode Copper. Her face was full of excitement. Bets and Jess stood among the other girls, waiting. I wished they both could win. They were so beautiful, inside and out.

"The Queen of the Rodeo is selected each season based upon her horsemanship, her character, and her willingness to learn," the announcer explained.

I chuckled at Red. He was rubbing his hands back and forth and whispering to the other clowns excitedly.

The master of ceremonies continued, "She is chosen out of all the rest to represent what is the heart and soul of rodeo—one who is a team player and who has a willingness to serve her fellow cowpokes."

"This is so exciting!" I heard Jess say.

"This young lady is all of these things and more. Please make welcome your new Cactusville Rodeo Queen . . ."

I crossed my fingers and closed my eyes.

"Moon . . . Holly . . . Soileau!"

"What? Did he say . . . me?" I looked at the clowns. They were cheering and holding up their hands in victory. "How could I be queen, Dango?" I looked down at my polka-dot duds. "I'm just a clown!"

"It doesn't matter how you serve, Moon Holly!" Dango answered. He grinned at me while tears spilled down his cheeks. "It only matters that you serve."

That did it! Now I was wiping my face, trying not to be sappy and cry all over myself. "Giddyap . . . I mean . . . Whoa, Glitter!" I sniffed all the way through the Grand Entrance.

Glitter trotted out into the arena as the audience rose to its feet. My head was spinning, but Lance River galloped alongside and acted as an escort for us. He laughed and stuck his hand out to congratulate me.

"You knew all along?" I asked.

Lance winked at me. "It was Buck and Dango's idea. They entered your name along with a letter signed by all your friends at the stables and by all the clowns. You won hands down, Moon!"

I shook my head. Even Bets and Jess knew. What neat friends I had! "I feel so goofy doing this in these clown clothes, Lance, and—" I felt my face "—my nose!" Except it sounded more like "by dose!"

Lance laughed. "God has a sense of humor."

A woman on horseback removed my clown hat, and another placed a cowgirl hat—the "crown"—on my head. It sparkled under the floodlights. I was so happy! Tears streaked down over the greasepaint on my face.

As Queen Moon, I would reign until the next rodeo. The Cactusville Rodeo gave me the most beautiful saddle I had ever seen. I didn't even care that I still didn't have a pony to strap it onto. I felt so good inside. Then I was presented with a two-week trip to the fancy dude ranch where Bets and Jess had been planning to go. "Wowee!" I cheered.

After the rodeo Bets and Jess hugged the stuffings out of me, and the clowns all slapped me five. Buck waited quietly until everyone had said their congratulations. His face looked serious.

"I need to have a talk with you, Moon," he said.

"Sure, Buck." I dismounted Glitter so Lance could lead her to the watering trough. "Is something wrong?"

"Someone offered to buy Glitter tonight, Moon. It was one of Dango's clowns. His name is Frisco. He wants Glitter for the star attraction."

"What?" I shook my head. This news couldn't be true! I felt like I had been socked in the stomach. "You sold Glitter?" I bit my lip. I didn't want to cry, but I couldn't help myself.

"Frisco is supposed to bring the money to buy her tomorrow. I told him I couldn't give him an answer until I talked to you."

"Is it more than a thousand dollars?" I peeled the nose off my face. I didn't feel funny anymore.

"A lot more than a thousand. Glitter is a trained trick pony now. But besides all that, she could make a lot of boys and girls happy. She's been invited to perform at a ranch for kids who have disabilities."

I burst into tears. God, please help me to be strong, I thought and nodded my head. "Then you have to sell her, Buck," I sobbed. "She can give those kids a smile. They need her more than I do." I couldn't believe my own words.

Buck hugged me and wiped tears from his own face too. "I know your heart must be breaking,

Little Bit. You've grown up a lot this week. You're
a special kid."

"I'm not special." I shook my head. "But Glitter's
special. That's why she has to go." I turned to walk
away. I wanted to hug her just one more time and give
her the carrot I had kept for her in my pocket.

"I need to ask you one more thing, Moon," Buck
added quickly.

"Yes?"

"Would you be willing to give up that saddle you
just won?"

Now God was *really* testing me. "Does Glitter need
it?" I asked.

"No, nothing like that, Moon. I have a certain colt
named Prince Ivy that's still for sale."

I whipped around to stare at him. "Prince Ivy?"

"If you twist my arm, you might be able to swap
that saddle for the colt."

I couldn't believe my ears! "Buck! You mean I can
buy Prince Ivy with a saddle?"

"That is exactly what I mean. That saddle is top-
notch, so it's a fair trade. You can train the colt yourself for rodeo competition, and you'll never outgrow
him. He has all the makings of a champion, Moon.
He's no trick pony."

I held out my hand to him. "I'll do it, Buck!"

"Congratulations, Miss Moon Holly Soileau! You're
an owner!" He shook my hand.

Bets and Jess came running up. "Tell us . . . what
did she say, Buck?" Bets yelled.

"She said yes!"

The girls whooped and hollered.

"Not only do you own a horse, but now you can go with us to the dude ranch, Moon!" Bets was so excited.

After I got dressed again, we prepared the horses to load them back into their trailers. I spent a lot of time rubbing down Glitter before loading her. Then Bets, Jess, and I schemed and giggled as we made plans for Prince Ivy. I finally had my dream—my own horse! Mom would never believe this story! God *was* good! But I couldn't help but wonder if I would ever love another horse as much as I loved Glitter.

The clown who was buying Glitter walked up behind me. I knew he was Frisco because I had remembered seeing him along with the others. Even without his clown makeup I knew it was him because he was the only clown my height. He was wiping his face with a towel. "Thanks for understanding about Glitter, Moon. As you can see, she's just my size."

I nodded and tried to smile.

"I'll be sure to write to you, Moon, and tell you how Glitter is doing. When I bring her back to Cactusville for the rodeos, I'll be sure to board her at Agape . . . as long as you're willing to be her stable hand."

"Thank you, Frisco!" What a clown! I felt better now. Maybe Glitter wouldn't forget about me, after all.

Behind the paddock a muddy pair of blue boots stuck out from under the railing. Elmer "Fuddsville" Higgins was at it again—eavesdropping. "I'll get even with that Moon Beam, yet!" he said to Todd.

"Now what?" Todd sighed.

"I don't know, but you can bet on one thing."

"What's that, Elmer?"

"I might just show up at that fancy-schmancy dude ranch myself. We've got the whole summer ahead of us, and I aim to make it miserable for that reject from Hollywood."

A strange look crossed Todd's face. "But, Elmer . . . Moon saved your life."

"She owed me! After all, I'm the one who *really* trained Glitter. She'll pay me back . . . or else!" Elmer stuffed a fist into his hand, and a snarl crossed his lips. "Nobody makes a fool out of Elmer Higgins . . . but nobody! Look out, Moon Beam! Here comes Elmer!"

"Oh, brother!" Todd shook his head.

Acknowledgments:

I wish to thank the fine people who were so help-ful in digging up the fine details that authenticate this book. Angela Williams of Maranatha Stables, Lou Bordelon of the Lazy B Stables, and Chris Jones of Live Oak Arabians—all true horsemen in their own right.

Also a special thank you to my editor, Alice Peppler. She saw the importance of this book first. I will always admire her understanding and expertise in fine tuning a novel for kids.

I would also like to extend a great big hug to the incredible kids at HCA elementary. They inspired me just when I needed a lift.